PENELOPE HENRY

Camping at Blueberry Mountain

Kathleen W. Forbes

PENELOPE HENRY: CAMPING AT BLUEBERRY MOUNTAIN
Copyright © 2016 by Kathleen W. Forbes

All rights reserved. Neither this publication nor any part of this publication may be reproduced or transmitted in any form or by any means, electronic or mechanical, including photocopying, recording or any information storage and retrieval system, without permission in writing from the author.

This is a work of fiction. Names, characters, places and incidents either are the product of the author's imagination or are used fictitiously, and any resemblance to actual persons, living or dead, businesses, companies, events, or locales is entirely coincidental.

ISBN: 978-1-4866-0797-6   Printed in Canada

Word Alive Press
131 Cordite Road, Winnipeg, MB R3W 1S1
www.wordalivepress.ca

Library and Archives Canada Cataloguing in Publication

Forbes, Kathleen W., 1930-, author
        Penelope Henry : camping at Blueberry Mountain / Kathleen W. Forbes.

Issued in print and electronic formats.
ISBN 978-1-4866-0797-6 (pbk.).--ISBN 978-1-4866-0798-3 (pdf).--
ISBN 978-1-4866-0799-0 (html).--ISBN 978-1-4866-0800-3 (epub)

        I. Title.

PS8611.O7215P47 2016   jC813'.6   C2015-901538-3
                                                C2015-901539-1

Contents

ACKNOWLEDGEMENT

My sincere thanks to Keith Beale for his beautiful illustrations in *Penelope Henry: Camping at Blueberry Mountain.*

SLOW DOWN, PENNY

Mr. Henry hammered the last nail into his old mare's shoe. "There, Tumbleweed, old pal," he said as he inspected his handiwork. "Now I can take the children on that camping trip I've been promising them! I always seem to have time for everyone else's horses, and I've put this job off far too long. I hope you'll forgive me, old girl. That shoe was beginning to hurt you, wasn't it?"

"Who are you talking to, Papa?" Penny asked as she bounded into the shop chasing a bright red ball which came to rest right under Tumbleweed.

The old mare flicked her tail as if to say, "Buzz off, Penny! It's my turn for some attention. Stop bothering me!"

Her papa smiled. "Well, you caught me! I guess this proves I'm getting old. I'm talking to old Tumbleweed here. It's not like she's going to answer me or anything. Yeah! That's a joke! Right, Tumbleweed, old girl?" He patted the horse affectionately on the rump.

"Of course I know what you're saying," Tumbleweed whinnied in her most disdainful horse language. "Kids! Humph!" She snorted as loud as she could to let them know she knew everything they said.

"All right, Tumbleweed! You don't have to make such a fuss!" Penny gave her a hug and stroked her nose to console her. "I brought you some sugar," she whispered as she dug her hand deep into her pocket. The old mare's ears perked up and she nuzzled her nose against Penny's arm, urging her to hurry.

Papa laughed. "Now look who's talking to the horse. I think she understands what you're saying to her. See how she nuzzles your hand?"

"That's because I'm the only one who ever brings her sugar. Isn't that right, Tumbleweed?"

The old horse answered with a soft whinny, shaking her head up and down as if in agreement. Penny whispered lovingly into her ear and told her what a wonderful horse she was as she petted the soft forelock. Tumbleweed nuzzled her head against Penny's neck.

"You sure have a way with her," her papa said. "Perhaps she'll be so grateful, she won't mind pulling the cart up to the Danby River. There's a nice little campground near Blueberry Mountain, and I think it's time we went for a weekend of fishing, adventure, and fun. Go tell Mama and your brother Zinger to start packing. We'll take the tent and stay for the weekend. We're taking the cart, because I don't think the old '67 Buick would make it over those mountain trails. Tell Mama I'll be home shortly. We'll pack all our camping gear into the cart, and if we hurry we should be able to start by noon."

Penny squealed with delight. She gave him a big hug and kissed Tumbleweed on the nose. "I love you, Papa, and thank you, thank you, thank you!"

Penny dashed out the door and almost collided with two strange men. The tall, skinny one wore a red bandana around his head, and the other was heavy and round like a barrel.

"Oh, sorry," Penny said quickly. Then she was off like a streak of greased lightning, singing at the top of her lungs to the tune of The Farmer in the Dell: "A-camping we will

4

go, a-camping we will go, we'll sing and play and swim all day, a-camping we will go!"

She sang loud enough for anyone and everyone in the village of Green Oaks to hear it.

In her excitement, she wasn't paying attention to anyone else and she ran right out in front of Mr. Wiggleby's bicycle.

"Watch out there, young Penny," Mr. Wiggleby shrieked as his bike careened wildly to the left and then to the right. He pulled on the handlebars to straighten out the wheels, all the while screaming with fright.

He finally landed in a bramble bush in Miss Sprightly's garden just as that dear lady was climbing down a ladder with a basket full of cherries she'd spent all morning picking. With a shrill piercing scream, she fell down and landed in a heap, scattering the cherries to the four winds.

Penny knew she was in trouble and was afraid to look. She peeked through her fingers and sighed. This was not good. Miss Sprightly was her schoolteacher.

"Oh my goodness! I'm s–so s–sorry, Mr. Wiggleby and Miss Sprightly," she stuttered. "I didn't mean to do that! Are you hurt? Please, please forgive me." She wanted to explain why she was in such a hurry, but knew it wasn't a good enough excuse for all the damage she had caused. "I was hurrying to tell Mama that Papa is going to take us camping."

She shuffled her feet and looked at the ground as she always did when she knew she'd misbehaved.

By now Miss Sprightly was on her feet and Mr. Wiggleby was trying to free himself from the bramble bush. He was grumbling, mumbling, and grouching about unruly children.

"Oh, my beautiful cherries!" Miss Sprightly moaned. "There goes the cherry pie I was looking forward to baking. Why don't you look where you're going, Penelope? And look at poor Mr. Wigglesby! He's covered from head to foot with brambles! Slow down young lady, or you'll cause a terrible accident!"

Penny hung her head in disgrace. "Sorry, ma'am!"

"Well, at least I didn't break any bones," Miss Sprightly said as she poked and prodded at her arms and legs. She checked the bones in her back as well, just to be sure.

Penny was afraid to look at Mr. Wigglesby as he continued to grumble about her behaviour.

"You'd better slow down!" he shouted at her, picking brambles out of his clothes. "Before you hurt someone!"

"Yes, sir." Penny felt truly guilty. "I promise I'll be more careful in the future."

Penny sighed woefully, noticing that neither one of them seemed to be the least bit excited about her camping trip.

She again started out, slowly at first, but soon she was running just like before, at full gallop, merrily singing her camping song. "A-camping we will go, a-camping we will go…"

Suddenly, there was a terrible racket as Penny's pet magpie, Blackie, zoomed in, excitedly flapping his wings. He shrieked in a continuous chatter as he landed on Penny's shoulder. He kept the ruckus up until Penny finally was able to calm him down by making soothing little clicking sounds with her tongue.

"It's okay, Blackie," she said. "You're coming, too. I wouldn't leave you behind. Let's go and tell Mama and Zinger!"

And now they were off like the wind again.

Penny saw Jill and Mandy on the street and waved gaily. The twin sisters were her best friends. "Hi, Jillybean. Hi, Mandy! We're going camping!"

Blackie soared high overhead and zoomed like a rocket between the girls, happily chattering.

"Camping, going camping," he screeched, breaking the girls up into peals of laughter.

"Have fun, Penny!" Mandy shouted after her. "Wish we were going with you!"

"Me too," said Penny. "Why don't you ask your mama if you can come too? We're leaving at noon. Well, must run."

Penny waved goodbye and was off again like a bullet. She tore around the corner of her street, singing her familiar song.

Suddenly, there was a dull, terrifying thud as she collided with Mrs. Turtledove, sending her parcels flying every which way. Apples rolled off in one direction and oranges went the other, while poor Mrs. Turtledove landed on her ample rear end with a frightening whoosh as the wind was knocked out of her.

Blackie screeched and swooped to a safe branch where he perched and surveyed the damage with his beady black eyes.

How am I going to explain this new disaster? Penny thought. She had better watch her step from now on. So far, this was not turning out to be a good day after all. What would Mama and Papa do when they heard about all the trouble she had caused? Perhaps Papa would change his mind about the camping trip. Penny sure hoped not.

"I am so sorry, Mrs. Turtledove," she wailed. "I've really done it this time. Mr. Wiggleby warned me to slow down or I would hurt somebody, and now I have! Please forgive me! Can I help you up?"

Penny realized she had been saying she was sorry a lot today. Mrs. Turtledove was her mama's best friend. Her mama would very likely hear about this, and Penny wondered what she would say.

"Nothing broken, I think, except perhaps a couple of eggs. How about helping an old woman up, will you, Penny?"

Penny pulled and tugged at Mrs. Turtledove. There was a lot of huffing and puffing, moaning and groaning, before Mrs. Turtledove managed to regain her footing if not her composure. Penny helped to dust her off, apologizing over and over again as she tried to explain why she had been running.

"Please don't be mad at me, Mrs. Turtledove."

"Well, no harm done this time, but you'd better slow down or you'll hurt somebody!"

"Slow down, slow down," mimicked Blackie from his regal perch on her shoulder.

Mrs. Henry stepped out of her cottage, wondering what the noise was all about. When she heard the story, she was horrified and worried about her old friend, but Mrs. Turtledove assured her that she was just fine.

"Oh, Mama, I'm so sorry," Penny said. "I was running to tell you and Zinger that Papa is taking us camping for the weekend. He told me to tell you to pack and be ready to go by noon."

Mama was as excited as Penny. "That's wonderful! I haven't been camping for years. But I will have a word with you later, young lady."

Penny sighed. "Uh–oh," she muttered to herself. "I'm in trouble again."

Mama was a round, jolly little woman whose smile crinkled up her whole face. She could move like lightning when the occasion demanded, though, and this was one of those occasions.

"Penny, go find your brother and we'll be packed and ready to go by the time Papa gets home. Watch that you don't run into anyone else on the way!"

Just then, six-year-old Zinger came crashing around the corner in his peddle car, their dog Frisky bounding along behind him.

"Stay right there, Zinger," Mama said. "We're going camping! Just as soon as we get ready." She turned to her old friend, Mrs. Turtledove. "I'm so sorry, my dear. Penny does get carried away sometimes, but she really is a good girl. Can I do anything to help you?"

"Oh, I'm fine," Mrs. Turtledove answered with a good-natured smile. "I do hope you have a lovely time camping!"

"That's very kind of you, dear."

They started off after lunch. The cart was packed with all sorts of goodies, and of course Papa packed his fishing gear, along with some new equipment he'd made in his workshop. No amount of coaxing could make him disclose what it was. All he would say was, "You'll find out when we get there."

They were just pulling out of the village and onto the main road when they heard shouts of protest behind them.

"Wait for us! Wait for us!" Jillybean and Mandy were kicking up dust as they tried to catch up.

"What's this?" Papa asked with one eyebrow raised.

"Oh, I was so excited, I forgot." Penny squirmed uncomfortably in her seat. "I'm sorry, Papa. I asked Jillybean and Mandy if they would like to come. I know I should have asked Mama first, but there wasn't time. Their mama must have given them permission to come."

"Yes, you should have asked Mama! What if there isn't enough food for everyone? We've also only packed two tents."

"Oh, there's plenty of food dear," Mama assured him. And there's also lots of room in the tents."

The two girls finally caught up. They had sleeping bags and backpacks with them.

"We thought we'd missed you," Jillybean panted. "Mama was at the market and we had to get her permission. We were all packed and ready when she got home. Thank goodness she agreed. And of course, I had to buy jellybeans for the trip. I thought we'd missed you."

Penny always called her "Jillybean" because she couldn't go anywhere without her jellybeans.

"Get in, girls," said Mama. "The more the merrier!"

Along the way, they came upon a very old man. His legs were crooked and he used a knobby stick to help him walk. He was bent over and seemed very weary, and he carried a heavy pack on this back with a fishing pole sticking out of it.

"Hello, friend," Papa said. "Would you like a ride?"

"I would, sir," the man replied. "I'd be truly thankful! The old legs are not what they used to be. Roby Kettle's the name."

"Pleased to make your acquaintance. I'm Thomas Henry and this is my wife, my son Zinger, and my daughter Penny. And these two young ladies are Penny's friends, Jill and Amanda."

Mr. Kettle nodded and made several attempts to get into the cart. He finally made it when Papa gave him a boost.

"Get over there, Frisky!" Papa ordered the dog. "Give the man some room!" Frisky waged his tail and curled up at the old man's feet. "That's better! Now we're full to overflowing."

They started on their way again and Penny started singing a round song. Soon everyone joined in, including Blackie. Tumbleweed clip-clopped along in time to the music.

Blackie swooped and soared around the cart, mimicking the few words he picked up from the singers. He kept everyone laughing each time he joined in with "Row, row, row your boat" or when he imitated the animals in Old McDonald's farm. The funniest part was when he crowed like a rooster. Even old Mr. Kettle was highly amused, and they all doubled over laughing. He was wonderful entertainment and made the trip seem shorter.

"Are we almost there yet?" Zinger asked, getting tired.

"Just a little farther, Zinger," Papa said.

"Oh! Look, everybody!" Penny pointed excitedly to the top of a huge tree. "There's a great big humongous bird up there. What kind of bird is that, Papa? See how it spreads its wings! See how wide they are!"

"My goodness! It's an eagle!" Papa exclaimed. "That's amazing! I had no idea they were so close to the village. Oh, look!" He pointed to the top of another tall tree. "There's another one!"

The children had never seen an eagle before, except in picture books. They had Zinger's attention now. They would have something exciting to tell their friends when they got home.

The weather was wonderful and there wasn't a cloud in the sky. Zinger finally settled down to enjoy the rest of the ride. But every now and then, he would gaze up into the trees to see if any more eagles were watching or following them.

"I don't know when I've ever enjoyed a camping trip more," old Mr. Kettle said. "I usually walk all the way to the Indian village with my friend, the old chief. Old Chief is retired now. His son Stormy is the new chief."

"Stormy?" Mama exclaimed. "What an odd name!"

"Yes," Mr. Kettle agreed. "You'll probably meet him at the campground. Nice young feller! Nice little family too."

The road was just a trail now and wound along the riverbank.

The journey took almost three hours, and the children were starting to get restless. As they pulled over the crest of a little hill, the campground came into view. It was a lovely little place, nestled in a grove of trees right beside the river. Tumbleweed seemed to know she had almost reached the end of her journey, and she fairly trotted the last hundred yards or so.

The children were off exploring before the cart had come to a full stop. Blackie swooped and zoomed from tree to tree, screeching and chattering with excitement. Frisky seemed to believe this was his very own playground. He chased a squirrel up a tree and then dared it to come down as he delightedly wagged his tail.

"If only I had half their energy," said Mr. Kettle. "I do thank you kindly for the ride, Mr. and Mrs. Henry! It's been a real pleasure to meet you and your family."

"You're very welcome, Mr. Kettle," Papa answered. "And if you want to ride back with us, just let us know."

"I may just do that. Thanks again!"

THE TALKING OWL

The children were delighted to discover there was a swimming hole, as well as barbecue pits and tables. At the other end of the campground, there was a slide and a row of swings.

Frisky made a beeline for the trees and vanished into them while old Mr. Kettle hobbled off along the riverbank to see his friend.

Zinger climbed a tree with branches reaching up to the sky, and he soon found a bird's nest.

"Look what I found, everybody!" he yelled. "It's a bird's nest! There are even tiny eggs in it!"

"Don't touch it!" The voice seemed to come from higher up in the tree and Zinger froze. Then a blood-curdling sound just above him terrified him even more.

"Wh–ho–oo–oo!"

Zinger shivered at the eerie sound.

"Who's th–there?" he stuttered, his eyes searching the branches for the offending voice. "Wh–where are you?"

"Up here," the voice commanded.

Zingers eyes scanned the foliage. All he could see was an old spotted owl peering at him with a scowl that told him he had better do as he was told.

Owls don't talk, he reasoned, but he was sure this one did and he wasn't about to stick around to find out for sure. He scrambled down the tree as fast as he could without falling down.

Stumbling and falling, howling and wailing in terror, Zinger ran as fast as his short legs would carry him toward the safety of his family's campsite. He hoped that whatever had scared him wouldn't decide to follow him.

Papa stopped what he was doing to stare in amazement at his son's dash for safety, but Mama could see that her son was really spooked.

"What in the world has gotten you so frightened?" she marvelled. "Come here, son, and tell me what has frightened you."

"Oh, Mama!" he cried. "I was so scared. An owl talked to me."

Papa threw his hands up in the air and roared with laughter. Mama couldn't help but join in until her whole body shook with the giggles.

"Ho–ho–ho, that's a good joke," Mama said. "An owl talked to Zinger!"

She was enjoying the joke until she got a good look at Zinger's horrified little face and realized this was no joke. She cuddled him close in her very best bear hug and tried to comfort him.

"But Mama," he wailed, "why did you laugh? I was scared!"

"I'm sorry, sweet boy. I shouldn't have laughed, but it sounded so funny. All right then. Why don't you tell us the whole story? Tell us why you think an owl talked to you."

Zinger told her what had happened.

Mama's face grew very solemn. "If someone or something told you not to touch the bird's nest, they were right. Do you know why?"

"N–no, Mama," Zinger said, still sniffling. "W–why?"

"Because if you had touched the nest, the mama bird would have abandoned the eggs and would never come back."

Zinger's face appeared even more horrified at this news, but he listened intently while Mama explained.

"So you see, sweet boy, whoever told you not to touch the nest did so to protect the eggs. Perhaps it was your conscience telling you not to do it. Besides, if you had fallen out of the tree, you might have broken a leg, or an arm, or something even worse."

Mama hugged her little warrior just a little tighter, and for the moment Zinger felt safe.

"What's a conscience, Mama?"

"It's the little voice in your head or your heart that tells you when something you are doing is right or wrong."

"But it really talked, Mama," he whispered. "I know the owl talked to me!"

"Let's talk about it later when Papa is all through setting up. Perhaps he can offer some words of wisdom to comfort you. Do you know where the girls are?"

"They're over by the swings."

Zinger seemed to have settled down, but every now and then his eyes couldn't help glancing up at the tree to see if he could see the owl. He shivered a little and wondered if he'd imagined it all. Sometimes funny things happened in dreams. Maybe this whole trip was just a dream! He wondered if he would dream tonight in the tent, and then he wished he was home in his own little bed.

"Call the girls, dear!" Mama said, breaking in on his daydream. "We'll have supper early and then you'll have time to explore."

"Okay, Mama."

He cautiously started across the campground, calling Penny's name. He didn't think he would be doing any exploring, at least not by himself, as he was fearful of the consequences. He was glad when he spotted the girls almost immediately.

Zinger wasn't usually afraid of his own shadow, but this was a whole different world to him. If he stayed close to Penny or Mama or Papa, he would be okay.

The girls had found a new friend, and Zinger wondered who she was. Penny introduced her as Summer. Penny said the girl lived in the Indian village. Her tribe owned the campground.

Funny name, he thought to himself.

•

Back at the campground, Papa whistled cheerfully. "Just about finished," he told his wife. "The tents are up and my new equipment is ready for the morning. I'd like to throw a line in after supper and check out the fishing. What a great spot this is." He spread his arms wide and made a complete turn. "Don't you think so, my dear?"

"It's wonderful for the children," his wife replied. "We really should do this more often. You work too hard, my dear husband!"

She had noticed how tired he was each evening after a long day's work, though he never complained. How she wished he would take life a little easier.

He was already building a fire in the barbecue pit. They would have hotdogs and lemonade for supper, and toasted marshmallows and hot chocolate before going to bed. She looked forward to their time around the campfire. Perhaps they would sing some campfire songs.

"I feel more rested already," Papa said. "Just getting away in the fresh air makes me feel like a young boy again.

I wonder what's keeping the children. They are always in such a hurry to eat!"

"Oh, here they come!" she told him. "And they've found a little friend already. Hm! How interesting. I didn't notice any other campers in the area. Did you, dear?"

"No, but then I was busy and didn't pay much attention."

"Mama! Papa!" Penny said excitedly. "We've found a friend who knows all about the river and the mountains. Her name is Summer Rain and she lives upstream, just around the bend in the river. Can she stay for supper?"

"Of course she can, dear!" Mama said. She was already setting a place at the table for their little guest. "How old are you, Summer?"

"I'm eight and a half, ma'am," the girl answered.

"Oh, how nice! Same age as Penny. Perhaps you'll become great friends. Won't you have to let your mama know you are staying with us for supper? She might be worried about you."

"My mama knows where I am, ma'am. My brother saw me coming here."

"Your brother?" Penny exclaimed. "I didn't see anyone else around."

"He's a little shy," Summer told her. "But he was there all right. You'll meet him later."

"Well, there's plenty of food, so you're welcome to stay, my dear," Mama said. "And we would love to meet your family."

"Oh, you will! My dada will be around to meet you later. Our tribe owns the campsite and Dada likes to know who is camping here."

"Wonderful!" Mama said. "We're eating early, because Papa wants to try his hand at fishing. He hasn't fished for years and he's so looking forward to it."

"I just wish I knew where to try my luck," Papa said. "Does your papa fish, Summer?"

"Dada loves to fish, and I can show you where the best fishing holes are. The rainbows are running and the best time is when the sun goes down, or before sunup, but you probably know that."

Papa smiled. "Not really, Summer. I seldom fish. I'm a real greenhorn, because I never seem to have the time. I will be thankful for any tips you can give me. Do you have any idea what kind of bait they use here?"

"My dada says worms are the best, but sometimes the fish will take bread or marshmallows," she said with a giggle.

"Marshmallows!" Zinger looked startled. "The fish can't have any of these marshmallows! There won't be any left after we toast them."

Everybody laughed and teased him, then pretended to put some away for the fish.

"Perhaps we'll just have to try it," Papa told him.

"That's the silliest thing I've ever heard," Zinger argued.

"Not any sillier than an owl that talks," Penny teased.

"Imagine giving marshmallows to a fish," Zinger said, "How would you like it, Penny, if we used your gummy bears for bait? I don't think you'd like that!"

"Okay, children, the wieners are just about ready," Mama told them. "Butter your bun and put all the trimmings on it. Just pretend you're family, Summer, and don't be shy!"

"Thank you, ma'am!" said Summer, making herself at home.

Mama smiled to herself at how delightful Summer was. Her beaded headband was very beautiful, and she wondered if Summer's mother had made it.

"Finish up your hotdogs and lemonade," Mama said to the children. "Then you can each look for a nice long stick for toasting marshmallows. They work best if you peel the bark off the end so you can easily pierce the marshmallow. I'll show you how. We did it when I was a girl."

"I'm going to find the best stick," Zinger shouted as he made a dash for the bushes. For the moment, the talking owl was forgotten.

"Don't be long, children," Mama said. "The sun will be going down soon and we want to use the fire while it's still nice and hot."

She cleared the dishes away while her husband started to attach the reel to his fishing pole.

"Now, where did I put that jar of worms?" her husband wondered.

"Don't worry, dear. I know where they are." She reached into the cart and discovered that the lid had come off the jar. Worms were crawling all over the place. "Oh no! Look at these horrible little wriggly, slimy things. You'll have to pick them up, dear. I can't bear to touch them."

She shivered at the thought.

Papa laughed merrily as he scooped up the offending fish bait.

Suddenly, the children were back, waving their sticks in the air.

"I found the best one. My stick is the best one!" Zinger sang out. "Look, everybody!" He showed it around and kept up his chant. "My stick's the best!"

Soon they were all telling him to be quiet.

"We found the perfect sticks," Penny announced proudly. "Summer showed us how to pare the end. See!"

The girls held their sticks up for inspection.

"Do mine too, Summer. Please!" Zinger pleaded.

"Sure, Zinger. See, it's easy! You pare it with the knife like this!" She demonstrated.

Mama was sure she had done it many times before.

"Very nice, indeed," Papa said approvingly. "All right, folks. While you toast your marshmallows, I'm going to try a little fishing. Where did you say was the best spot, Summer?"

"You can try over there by that large oak tree, Mr. Henry. My dada always likes that spot. The fish love the shade."

"I'll take your word for it. Thank you, my dear! Well, wish me luck!"

"Good luck, Papa!" Penny shouted after him.

Mama hadn't seen her husband so relaxed in a long time and the children seemed to be enjoying themselves. They would learn a lot about nature, and she was sure this was going to be a lovely holiday.

When she found just the right stick, she joined the others at the fire. She showed the children how to toast the marshmallows, though Summer was way ahead of them.

"Anybody know some good campfire stories?" Penny asked.

"How about ghost stories?" Zinger teased.

"You're getting awfully brave, Zinger," Penny said. "I'm afraid of ghost stories myself, because somebody had to die to become a ghost."

"They scare me too!" Jillybean said. "What about you, Summer? Do you know any good stories?"

"Well, my grandmother heard this story from her great-great-grandma. I think that makes her my great-great-great-great-grandma. I call her great-grandma four. When great-grandma four was a little girl, she lived in a tepee with her mama and papa and brother and sister."

"What's a tepee?" Zinger asked.

"Hush, Zinger," Penny scolded.

"A tepee is a big tent shaped like an ice cream cone," Summer explained. "It's made of animal skins, like elk, or buckskin, same as my slippers. My slippers are called moccasins. The earthen floor is usually covered with buffalo hides or bear skins to keep everybody nice and warm. There is always a fire in the middle of the tepee in the cold weather and the logs are stacked standing up, like a cone, so that the smoke will rise and escape through the hole at the top of the tepee."

"You mean people back then didn't live in cottages like we do?" Penny asked.

"No, the tepee was their home and they were very warm and cozy. There was a whole village of tepees here then, and everyone took care of each other. We don't live in tepees anymore, except for old Chief White Feather. He has a tepee and won't live in a cabin. He still prefers the old ways, and because he's so old, he probably will never change. Sometimes my grandpa stays with him just to keep him company. Nobody knows how old Chief White Feather is.

"One day, some bandits rode in and burned the village down, but great-grandma four and great-grandpa four escaped with the children through a hole they cut in the back of the tepee. They crawled away on their stomachs like cougars and made it to the woods.

"They hid for three days because they were afraid the bandits would come back. Some of the tribe escaped

to Blueberry Mountain, and after a few days they came back to help the ones who were still hiding. They brought food and extra ponies, and when everyone had eaten, they joined the tribe in a new hiding place in the mountains where they stayed until it was safe for them to come back and set up a new village."

The children's eyes were wide with fright.

Mama was shocked. "How could the bandits be so cruel?"

"Most of the families got away," said Summer. "But some of the braves died trying to protect their families. The bandits finally left when the village was destroyed. Sometimes, when the moon is full, they say you can see the braves' ghosts riding, in full headdress, fighting to protect the village."

"That is the most scary ghost story I have ever heard!" said Penny, and the other girls agreed with her. "Did the bandits ever get caught and punished?"

"Yes, it took the soldiers a long time to find them, but they were caught and punished."

"What happened to them?" Penny asked.

"Grandma said I was too young to know everything. She said that when I am older, she will tell me the rest of it."

"I would be so scared if that happened to me," said Jillybean. "I wouldn't know what to do."

"Neither would I," Penny agreed.

"What a sad story," Mama said. "Well, thank goodness your great-grandma four and great-grandpa four were saved, or we would never have met you, Summer. Did your tribe set up homes on the same land as before, or did they find another location?"

"As soon as they knew they were safe, they came back down to the same spot where we have our village today. It wasn't long before they made new tepees."

"I would like to live in a tepee," Zinger said.

"Why is that?" Mama asked.

"Because it would be like camping all the time. Wouldn't that be fun? We could toast marshmallows every night and have wieners on the barbecue for hotdogs and Papa could go fishing every day. I think that would be really neat!"

"Oh, you do?" Mama laughed. "I think you would find it a bit cold in the winter, but I suppose it does sound like fun to a six-year-old."

Suddenly, they all heard a triumphant yell that seemed to come from the direction of the big oak tree. A voice that was terrifyingly familiar to Zinger called out loud and clear across the clearing: "Who–oo–oo, who–oo–oo. Who!"

"Wh–what w–was th–that?" Zinger said, barely whispering. "D–did you hear that, Mama?" His eyes were wide and he shivered in fright. He made a beeline for the safety of his mama's arms.

"It's all right, Zinger," Mama consoled him. "It was just Papa shouting. He must have caught a fish."

"No, Mama!" he wailed. "It was the other voice. Didn't you hear it? It shouted real loud. Who–who–who–oo…" Zinger's voice trailed off to a whisper again.

Summer and Mama laughed gleefully again, but Penny and the other girls weren't so sure if they should.

Zinger's lip trembled. He couldn't understand why they were laughing at him. The voice was really scary.

NATURE AND ANIMALS

Penny looked bewildered. "What was that?" she asked with a puzzled frown.

"That was an owl, silly girl," Mama said, still chuckling. "Oh, don't tell me you children have never heard an owl before!"

"You mean, that was Zinger's talking owl?" Penny asked.

"I'll get my brother Wolfie to show Zinger some of the animals tomorrow, then he won't be so frightened," Summer said. "I suppose if you have never lived near the rivers or mountains, you haven't had the chance to learn about animals and nature. Don't worry, Zinger! By the time you leave to go home, you will have seen lots of animals."

Zinger wasn't so sure he wanted to see any more animals.

"They won't hurt you, I promise," Summer assured him. "They are more afraid of you than you are of them.

You and Wolfie should get along real well. He is the same age as you!"

"He is?" Now Summer had Zinger's attention. "Isn't he afraid to explore the woods by himself?"

"No! This is where we were born and we've lived here all our lives. We know all about the woods and the animals that live here. If you like, we will show you around tomorrow."

"Wow! That would be super!"

Penny and the girls agreed.

Mama liked the way Summer had calmed Zinger down and was amazed at how clever she was for one so young.

"You seem so much older and wiser than an eight-year-old," she told Summer.

Summer straightened up. "Eight and a half, ma'am."

"Oh yes, of course! Eight and a half. That does make a difference." Mama smiled to herself. Such a clever girl, she thought. "Well, shall we go and see what Papa was shouting about?"

Sure enough, when they reached the riverbank, Papa was cleaning a huge fish.

"Oh! That's a real nice rainbow trout," Summer exclaimed.

Papa grinned from ear to ear with pride. "Yes, I've never caught such a big fish. It must be about eight pounds. There'll be enough for all of us for tomorrow's dinner."

Penny clapped her hands with delight. She had never seen her papa so pleased and happy. "That's good fishing, Papa!"

Just then, a man and a small boy entered the clearing. Mama got the impression that they were related to Summer.

"I think we have some company," Mama remarked.

"Summer, I told you not to bother the campers," the man said. "Hi, folks! I hope she hasn't been any trouble."

"Trouble? Not at all," said Papa. "She told me where to fish and I caught a real beauty. She's a fountain of information. I take it you're Summer's father!"

"Yes. My name is Storm Cloud. Just call me Stormy! Everybody does. And this is my son, Silver Wolf. He answers to Wolf. Are you enjoying your campout?"

"Yes, indeed," said Papa. "Nice to meet you, Stormy. My name is Thomas Henry, and this is my wife Mary. These are my children, Penny and Zinger, and those two sweet little girls are Penny's friends, Jill and Amanda. Please, won't you join us around the fire? I'd like to know more about this camp. It's so beautiful here and peaceful."

They spent the next hour cooking marshmallows, eating chips, and drinking lemonade. They told each other about their lives. Stormy told them that his tribe owned the land all the way up into the foothills of Blueberry Mountain. They allowed anyone to use the campground as long as they took care of their own clean-up and didn't harm the animals.

"As First Nations tribe leaders, we believe we are care-takers of the land," Stormy said. "We believe it should always be kept wild and free for the animals that live here. I decided to set up the campground so people could get away from civilization for a little while to enjoy nature. So far, it has worked out quite well, and the people who come have been respectful and grateful."

"Would it be okay if I tried to work a little portable sluice in the river?" Papa asked. "I really don't know how to use it, but I've always wanted to try."

So that's what that special equipment is that Papa brought, Penny thought to herself. But what's a sluice?

Stormy told Papa to go right ahead and even gave him some pointers on the basics. "Dig under the black sand along the riverbank. The black sand is full of magnetite, which is heavy, but the gold is heavier and sinks below. It's good for prospecting. Sometimes you can find gold dust or small particles up to the size of oatmeal, and the sandbar at the bend of the river has some nice coloured gemstones in it. My wife makes beautiful jewellery with them."

"Is that so?" Papa sounded excited. "The girls will be happy to hear that. Thank you very much, Stormy."

Stormy laughed. "Almost everyone who comes up here hopes to find their fortune. Some people come with pans and sit in the river all day shaking the dirt out. If they find anything, they are welcome to it. Personally, I would rather fish!"

"Well, I'm going to try in the morning, just for fun," Papa told him. "If I find something, it will be a bonus. If I don't, it doesn't matter. I'm enjoying the fun and beauty of this place."

"Life is too short, my friend," Stormy told him. "Take time to enjoy nature. You'll never be sorry."

Papa gazed thoughtfully up and down the river. "Did you happen to see an old man fishing around the bend?" he asked. "He came with us, but we haven't seen him since we arrived. I wonder if he is okay."

"Oh yes. You must mean old Roby Kettle. He comes here a lot. He's visiting old Chief White Feather. They've been friends for years."

A bit farther down the riverbank, Zinger and Wolf had become great friends. They skipped flat stones across the water to see who could skip them the farthest. Meanwhile, Summer and the girls were making plans for the next day. They had lots to do and wanted to start out bright and early.

Mama watched them with a contented smile and then decided it was time for everyone to go to bed. They were more than ready. They'd had a very exciting day and were looking forward to the next morning.

The three girls shared a tent while Zinger bunked in with Mama and Papa.

That night, they all fell asleep to the sound of the rushing river and the nightingale's song. Scurrying little night creatures darted here and there, and the faint,

haunting sound of faraway violin music lulled everyone into a peaceful dreamland.

Zinger dreamed of a talking owl, and Penny dreamed of her newfound friend, Summer. Jillybean and Mandy were so tired that they simply crashed.

Papa lay awake for a long time. What a great day, he thought. He decided that they would do this again some-time soon. The road to the campground hadn't been as bad as he had thought it would be. He could have brought the Buick. Still, it was more fun coming by cart. They might not have noticed the eagles if they'd been riding in the car.

He hoped the sluice would work—if he could only figure out how to use it. The fish he had caught was the biggest he had ever seen. He would certainly have a fish-erman's tale to tell his friends in Green Oaks. Even the children were having more fun than they'd ever had before.

As he settled himself comfortably and yawned, he wondered if he would fall asleep. He was impatient for the morning to arrive, but soon he was caught up in a magical dream, fancying that he had found his fortune in gold.

The children awoke to the sounds of rattling pans and dishes. They peeked out of the tent flaps to find Mama happily flipping pancakes. Tumbleweed was contentedly grazing nearby and Blackie waited patiently for Penny to make an appearance. Frisky's tail was wagging at the prospect of eating breakfast. But Papa was nowhere in sight.

"Where did Papa go?" Zinger asked.

"To the sandbar at the bend of the river," Mama told him. "He set up his sluice early this morning."

Jillybean and Mandy were rubbing the sleep out of their eyes and yawning.

"Come on, you two sleepyheads!" she urged them. "You'd better get dressed. Breakfast is almost ready."

"What's a sluice?" Penny asked her mother.

"You will have to ask Papa to explain it to you," Mama said. "He will be here in a few minutes, and both you and Zinger aren't dressed yet. Don't forget to wash

"What does it do, Papa?" Zinger inquired.

"Well, if it works, son, and if we're lucky, we just might find gold!"

Just then, Stormy arrived, and he showed Papa how to work his sluice. He dug the black sand out of the riverbank and sandbar, then washed it down the sluice with water from the river. Stormy explained that if there was gold, the riffles and rough carpet would trap it. It seemed to be a lot of work to Penny and the girls, and they soon lost interest and went in search of the pretty stones Summer had told them about.

The sandbar, which the sun had turned into a dazzling spectrum of colour, was just waiting to be discovered by three awestruck girls.

"Look here, Penny. Here's one with red and white stripes. Isn't it pretty? Oh, and look at this one!" Summer held up a shining amber-coloured stone. "This is a tiger's eye!"

"Oh wow! These are so awesome!" Penny was getting excited now. "Here is one that looks like a diamond! These are better than gold. Don't you think so, Summer?"

Penny was sure she had discovered her fortune!

"That looks like crystal," Summer told her.

Jillybean and Mandy discovered some pretty agates, jade, and topaz, and they filled their pockets in no time. Summer knew all the names of the different stones.

The girls gathered as many beautiful gemstones as their pockets would hold.

"I wish we had brought something to carry them in," said Mandy. "I've never seen anything so fine."

The boys had also lost interest in the sluice and went into the woods to find some animals.

"Let's hide behind this bush," Wolf told Zinger. "And if we are real quiet, we might see some deer."

Sure enough, there was a slight rustle in the bushes before long and a tiny baby deer staggered into the clearing with its mama doe. For once, Zinger was speechless. All he could manage was a whispered "Oh...oo."

Suddenly, a whole flock of wild turkeys crashed through the bushes and headed straight for Zinger and Wolf. They were going "Gobble-gobble-gobble" and Zinger thought they were going to gobble him up. With a shriek of terror, he turned and ran for the river, with Wolf following close behind him.

"They're going to eat us!" wailed Zinger.

"No they're not!" Wolf tried to assure him.

Poor Zinger was scared to death. "I heard them. They said they were going to gobble me."

Wolf laughed hysterically. "They're as frightened of you as you are of them."

Zinger still wasn't convinced.

They both jumped in fright as a jubilant yell reached them from the direction of the river. The deer and turkeys bolted in the other direction and the boys ran for the river, only to collide with Penny and the girls.

"Something terrible has happened to Papa!" Penny exclaimed. "What is it, Papa?"

All five of them ran to where they'd left Stormy and Papa.

"I've found it!" Papa shouted. "I've found it!"

"What did you find, Papa?" Penny still felt a little cautious and puzzled, but she noticed that he seemed to be very happy. He was holding something in his hand and grinning from ear to ear.

"I've found our fortune!" he shouted as he showed them a huge gold nugget half the size of his fist.

Stormy came running up and was really pleased when he saw that his new friend had found his dream. "Good for you, Mr. Henry," he said. "But personally, I would rather fish."

Mama heard the shouting and ran over to find that her husband had caught more than a fish this time. He was so excited that he was almost ready to burst his buttons.

"We're rich! We're rich!" he shouted happily at the top of his lungs.

Penny and Zinger jumped up and down, singing gleefully with their father.

Blackie screeched in a wild frenzy as he swooped and zoomed above the jubilant group. "We're rich! We're rich! We're rich!"

Jillybean and Mandy looked at each other and shook their heads, thinking everyone had gone mad.

"What's the big deal?" Jillybean asked. "It's just a rock."

"I'll be able to take it easy for a while," said Papa. "And Mama can buy new clothes. I wonder how much it's worth." He had visions of endless wealth.

Stormy examined it carefully. "There is a nice solid vein of gold running through it, but you'll have to take it to the assayer's office in Green Oaks. He'll be able to tell you how much it's worth. It's the biggest one I've ever seen, but don't count your chickens just yet. Congratulations, my friend, on a real lucky find."

"That's a funny thing to say," said Zinger. "We don't have any chickens to count!"

"It doesn't matter how much it's worth," Papa declared. "This is the best holiday we've ever had, and it's not over yet. I found my gold, Zinger spoke to a talking owl, and we met wonderful friends."

"And a whole flock of turkeys wanted to eat me," wailed Zinger. Now that the excitement about the gold was over, he tried to get somebody's attention, but nobody was listening.

"And we have fish for dinner," said Mama. "Yes, I would say this has indeed been the best holiday."

"What's this about a talking owl and turkeys wanting to eat Zinger?" Stormy asked.

Suddenly someone had paid attention to Zinger, so he told his story. He frowned, however, when he saw Wolf rolling on the ground, howling with laughter.

"What's so funny?" asked Zinger with a puzzled frown.

"You are, Zinger! Oh... oh... I can't stop laughing!" Wolf held his stomach as he tried to explain. "The owl wasn't talking, Zinger. That was me! I was up very high in the tree when I saw you reaching for the bird's nest, and I yelled over to stop you."

"That was you? But I heard it saying 'Who, who,' and in the evening when we were around the campfire, I heard it again!"

Wolf had calmed down by now, especially after Stormy gave him one of his severe looks.

"Sure!" Wolf said. "That's the call owls make. All the birds make a different call."

"But what about the turkeys that wanted to gobble me?" Zinger asked.

"Gobble-gobble is the sound a turkey makes. Every animal makes a different call."

"Gobble-gobble-gobble," shrieked Blackie.

"Make Blackie stop that, Penny," Zinger pleaded.

"Now I know I have to bring my children camping again," Papa said. "And often. I didn't realize they knew so little about birds and animals."

"Well, you're welcome to come here anytime, my friend," Stormy told him. "I hope you make it soon."

"I'm sorry, Zinger," Wolf apologized. "I know I shouldn't have laughed at you." He still chuckled softly to himself, grinning from ear to ear. Every now and then, he would burst into gales of laughter and clamp his hand over his mouth to stifle the noise.

"Mama, Summer is going to take us into her village to show us a tepee," Penny said. "And then we're going to explore a cave. Can we go?"

"Well, the village sounds fine, but the cave might be dangerous."

"Oh, don't worry," Stormy assured her. "Summer knows every inch of the cave. They'll be fine."

After a warning from Mama not to be late for supper, and an invitation for Summer and her family to join them for their evening meal, the children raced each other along the riverbank. They followed the well-worn path, stopping every now and then to explore the hollow bases of the enormous trees with their gnarled, twisted roots and cave-like recesses.

"What a great place to play hide and seek," said Penny. "This one would make a great treehouse."

"It is a treehouse!" Summer told her. "Dinty Finnigan lives here."

"Who's Dinty Finnigan?" Penny asked.

"He's a tiny little elf from the fairy kingdom. He calls himself a leprechaun, and he's probably watching us right now. So we'd better not hang around here." Summer looked around, half-expecting him to pop up. The children were delighted.

"Does he have a family?" Zinger's eyes were wide and his face was beaming. "I mean, does he have leprechaun children?"

"Yes! But very few people have seen them. Only the little children, and only if they are in trouble. That's when Dinty and his friends show themselves to help the little one who needs to be rescued."

"Have you ever seen him?" Penny asked.

"Only once, when I was about four. I fell into a badger hole and couldn't get out. Dinty and his friends pulled me out. Dinty took my hand and walked me home."

"Were you afraid of him?" Jillybean asked.

"No! He was smaller than me, but he was very kind. He helped my cousin Buck when he fell into the river a couple of months ago. Buck is only three and he would have drowned if Dinty hadn't seen him. So he's a good leprechaun. Many times we've heard their music at night. Sometimes they play the violins and dance all night long."

"Well, I think we should get out of his house," Wolf warned them. "Just in case he gets mad at us and uses magic to chase us away."

They all scrambled out of the tree trunk and ran down the path towards the village.

When they arrived, a crowd of little kids followed them to the tepee. It was the biggest tent Penny and Zinger had ever seen, and it was everything Summer had described in her story. When they stepped inside, Penny couldn't believe how much room there was. It was as big as her own house, except a lot higher.

Summer introduced them to her grandfather, who shared the tepee with old Chief White Feather, and he allowed them each to choose one of his hand-carved animals. Zinger chose a deer and Penny an eagle. Jillybean chose a bear and Mandy a fox.

Summer's mama showed them how she made jewellery with the gems she found in the riverbed and gave each of them a beautiful pendant. She gave Zinger a small box decorated with the gem stones. Zinger was entranced with the box and said he would keep his special things in it. She also gave them some lunch, and then they followed Wolf and Summer again, this time beyond the village.

"What's that noise?" Penny asked.

"That's the waterfall," Summer said. "It's just through the trees there, and the cave is behind it."

When the waterfall came into view, they all gasped.

"Oh, it's so awesome!" Penny exclaimed.

"This is the best!" Jillybean agreed.

Wolf and Zinger ran on ahead and soon disappeared from sight.

"Where did they go?" the girls all wondered aloud.

"Oh, they've just gone into the cave," Summer told them. "Follow me and watch that you don't slip."

They reached the edge of the waterfall and Summer stepped onto a ledge.

"Stay close to me," she said. "Take my hand, Penny, and hang on to Jillybean. Jillybean can take Mandy's hand. Step behind the waterfall, like this!"

The girls screamed with fright a few times. Suddenly, they were in the cave, and there they saw Wolf and

Zinger. But they weren't alone. Two other people stood in the cave. Penny and her friends were frightened until their eyes adjusted.

When they could finally see in the dim light behind the falls, they saw the faces of two old men—and one of them was Mr. Kettle. Penny breathed a sigh of relief. The men were sitting on blankets in front of a log fire.

"Hi there, Summer," said the oldest looking man Penny had ever seen. He grinned at them and Penny noticed he hadn't a single tooth in his mouth. His white hair fell down to his waist and he wore buckskin pants and a vest. He had a blanket around his bent shoulders.

Mr. Kettle nodded when he saw the kids. He looked right at home. Both men seemed happy to see them.

"Came to see old Chief, did you, Summer gal?" Mr. Kettle said. "And who are your friends? Come over here so I can get a good look at you. The old eyes aren't so good these days."

Summer introduced everyone and then added, "This is Chief White Feather, and Mr. Kettle is his friend."

"Happy to meet you all," the old chief greeted them. "If you're hungry, I've got some smoked fish jerky. Pass some around, Summer."

Soon they all had a piece of smoked fish jerky.

"It's delicious," Penny exclaimed, and the others all agreed. "I've never tasted smoked fish before. How long were you the chief, sir?"

"So long that I don't remember. The new chief is Storm Cloud. I'm too old to make decisions for the tribe. Stormy was educated in the white man's university and can deal with the white man's laws. I just like to fish and whittle these days. But thank you for coming to visit me. Roby comes to see me once in a while. I'm glad of the company! Come back and see me at my tepee!"

"We'd better go now," said Summer. "I promised to get them home in time for supper. Mr. and Mrs. Henry have invited our family to have supper with them. Thanks for the jerky."

When they arrived back at the campsite, they were full of excitement about the day's adventures. Mama had started supper and was looking forward to their fireside stories.

"You can tell us about your day after supper when we're sitting around the campfire," she said. "Now, everybody wash up! Summer and Wolf's parents will be here any minute. Oh, here they come now."

Stormy and his wife arrived with a smoked fish, salad, and dessert.

"This is my wife, Autumn Wind," Stormy said, introducing her to everybody. "And these are the new friends I have been telling you about, Mr. and Mrs. Thomas Henry and their family and friends. You've already met the children earlier today."

"I'm very happy to meet you," Autumn Wind greeted them. "Summer and Wolf have been so excited to make new friends, and they've been telling me some interesting stories about a talking owl and turkeys that eat you. I just had to come and hear for myself."

"We are very pleased you could join us," Mama told them. "Oh, the smoked dish and salad look delicious, and don't tell me this is blueberry pie! How wonderful! Thank you very much indeed. We don't expect to eat in such a grand manner when we are camping. It will be difficult to go back to hotdogs and hamburgers tomorrow, but tonight we have two kinds of fish—smoke and fresh-caught—and this wonderful pie, for which we are truly thankful."

Stormy and Papa pulled another table over to make

enough room for everyone, and soon they were all seated.

Mama beamed as she looked on all the happy faces. "This is the easiest meal I've made since we got here. All I had to do was throw the fish on the barbecue!"

"We were going to go back home tomorrow," said Papa. "But I've decided we will stay over until Monday morning. We'll leave early and get home before noon. This is the first time I've taken any time off in five years and I feel like a young man again."

"You are a young man, my dear," his wife told him. "You just need to take time to relax."

"Papa's rich now," said Penny. "He found his fortune today, and maybe he'll find more gold tomorrow. We found our fortunes too, these beautiful stones for making jewellery!"

"Oh, I think I've done all the prospecting I'm going to do this weekend," Papa said. "I think I'll just fish tomorrow."

"That's what I say," said Stormy. "Maybe I'll join you, if you don't mind."

Papa was delighted. "Splendid!"

"Well, since we're not going home tomorrow, let's plan what we are going to do," Penny suggested.

"Oh yes, let's," Jillybean agreed. "Do you have any ideas, Summer? I mean, you know everything there is to do around here."

"Let me think about it for a while," Summer told them. "Don't worry! I'll think of something. Can you swim?"

"I can," said Penny. "And Jillybean and Mandy can too. We're not bad swimmers, but Zinger can't swim a stroke. He hasn't had the chance to learn yet."

"There's a nice swimming hole just past the campground. We could do that, but I'll put my thinking cap on and show you how to have fun in the wilderness."

"I want to see the leprechauns," said Zinger.

"They only show themselves when they want to. You see, they can make themselves invisible. They don't have wings like a fairy, but they have the power to jump very high and dart about as fast as lightning. They can also make themselves very small if it's necessary. It's all done by magic."

"I want to see Dinty," said Zinger.

"Well, I can't do anything about that," Summer said. "But for anybody who gets himself into trouble as much as you do, like getting chased by wild turkeys, you just never know."

"Okay, children, I see Papa has almost got the campfire ready," Mama said. "Let's clear the dishes and get ready to tell us what you did today. Maybe we'll sing some campfire songs."

There was much excitement around the campfire as they told the adults all about the tepee and the cave. Zinger couldn't seem to think about anything except Dinty Finnigan and his treehouse. The girls were wearing the beautiful pendants that Autumn Wind had given them, and they showed how they were made.

"What's this about leprechauns?" Papa inquired.

So Penny told her father what Summer had told them about Dinty Finnigan. "Isn't that exciting, Papa?"

"I don't know!" he said. "Aren't leprechauns supposed to live in Ireland, er... that is, if they are real?"

"That's true," said Summer. "They say that Dinty and some friends heard some beautiful music one night, and they grabbed their violins and followed it right onto a big ship. They danced and played the night away and then fell asleep. When they woke up, the ship was out on the sea. Nobody on the ship had seen them because they were in-

visible. So that's how they got to this country. He does like it here, but someday he'll go home the same way he came. He misses his kin."

"That's quite a story!" Papa winked at Stormy and was quite surprised that he didn't wink back.

Mama admired Autumn Wind's beautiful black hair. It cascaded over her shoulders like a silk velvet shawl and her golden brown skin was like soft satin. When she smiled, her coal-black eyes sparkled like shining stars. She was the most beautiful woman Mama had ever seen, and she couldn't help noticing how Summer looked just like her.

A couple of tiny squirrels timidly approached Wolf and took the popcorn he offered them. The children were speechless with enchantment.

Summer snuggled close to her mother while they toasted the remaining marshmallows over the campfire. As the sun went down over Blueberry Mountain, its red, yellow, and golden magic twinkling and dancing over the water like mischievous fairy sprites, the two families knew they would remain good friends forever. Storm Cloud and his family were invited to visit whenever they came to town.

THE RESCUE

The sun was bright and the sky an azure blue. It was going to be a lovely day. At least, Penny thought so.

Summer and Wolf came over early. They had just finished their breakfast and were raring to go.

Papa and Stormy had been out fishing for a couple of hours and the kids wore their swimsuits. Summer and Wolf had brought beach balls and were in the process of hanging a net between the trees along the riverbank. Autumn Wind came to invite Mama to go for a walk to the village.

The kids chose sides and played beach ball for a couple of hours. Because Zinger's and Wolf's legs were so short, they spent a lot of time falling on their faces while trying to reach the ball. Blackie was having a great time. Every time the ball was in flight, Blackie tried to catch it, screeching as loud as he could.

"Catch it, Blackie!" Penny shouted.

They all burst into gales of laughter when Blackie mimicked her in a harsh screech: "Catch it Blackie, catch it Blackie!" And all the while he chased frantically after the ball.

By now Zinger and Wolf were fed up with the game and decided to try out the water. They grabbed a towel each and wandered off on their own. The swimming hole was too deep for Zinger, so they decided to go to the sandbar. The water was shallow and calm and they played and splashed about for a while. Wolf didn't notice that Zinger was slowly working his way out towards the fast water, and he stepped into a hole. The water came up over his head.

He bounced up and screamed in terror as he thrashed around helplessly. Then he went under again. Wolf yelled for help, afraid to go into the fast water.

Suddenly, as Zinger bounced up again, a strong arm grabbed him and pulled him into the quiet water.

"Come on, wee fellow! Get up now! You're too big to carry. Hey there, Wolfie! Come and give us a hand. There's a good lad!"

"Dinty?" Wolf ran towards him. "I'm coming! Hang on to him, Dinty!"

Wolf grabbed Zinger's other shoulder, and he and Dinty pulled a half-drowned Zinger to safety.

"Sit on his chest there, Wolfie, and bounce up and down 'til he gets rid of the water. You're heavier than I am. There, that's it!"

Zinger started to spit water up. When he looked up, he was suddenly aware of Wolf and Dinty. His eyes opened wide. "Get off me, Wolf! You're killing me!"

"He's saving your life, Zinger m' lad," Dinty said. "I heard you wanted to meet me, but you didn't have to drown yourself to do it. I'm Dinty Finnigan, at your service, m'boy!"

"D–dinty Finnigan? R–really?" Zinger was awestruck. "You saved me, Dinty, didn't you?"

"Well, Wolfie here had something to do with it too. You should learn to swim before you go out into the fast water. And even then, you're better to stay in calm water. Oh, oh, I've got to go. The big fellows are coming. And stay out of m' treehouse, you hear me?"

"Y–yes, Dinty. Thank you for saving me," Zinger stammered. "I'll never forget you."

"Yes you will, me lad. Just as soon as you grow up! Goodbye, boys, and be more careful in the water." And with a whoosh, he vanished.

"Zinger!" Penny ran toward them, shouting in alarm. "We heard you screaming. Are you all right?"

"I am now! I fell into a deep hole in the fast water, and I would have drowned if Dinty Finnigan and Wolfie hadn't saved me."

"Where is he? I don't see him!" Penny and the girls looked all around them, but couldn't find Dinty. "You must have been dreaming, Zinger. He's not here!"

"I know he's not here," Zinger said, feeling better now. He was proud that only really little kids, like him and Wolfie, could see his hero. "He's not here because he doesn't let the big kids see him. Wolfie saw him and helped Dinty pull me out of the water. Isn't that right, Wolfie?"

"That's right. And he knew my name. He called me Wolfie, and he knew Zinger's name too."

"He's probably watching us right now," said Summer. "He can make himself invisible and knows everything that goes on here."

"Thank you, Dinty!" Penny shouted. "I wish I could see you to thank you, but I'm glad you were here for Zinger."

"Nobody will believe this if we tell them," said Mandy. "Maybe we should be quiet about it."

"Well, I'm not going to be quiet," said Zinger. "He's my friend and my hero and he saved me."

"You're all crazy. Little men," Jillybean muttered. "Little leprechauns! Hah!"

Mama spotted the kids on her way back from the village. "Hi there!" she called. "I'll be making lunch in a few minutes. Just hotdogs! Ten minutes! It will be ready by then. Wash up while you're at the river."

"Okay, Mama!" Penny said. "And thank you, Wolf, for helping Dinty to save my brother. Zinger's a pest sometimes, but I love him and I don't know what I'd do if we lost him."

Wolf answered her with a shy smile.

Zinger gave his big sister a hug. "I love you too, Penny," he whispered.

"Well, let's go! Lunch is ready and we've got lots to do yet today," Penny said as she headed back to the tent.

They all grabbed a hotdog and lemonade and quickly went to work on them. They didn't want to waste any time, since this was their last day.

"What are you girls planning to do this afternoon?" Mama asked.

"I thought we would go for another swim at the swimming hole, and then maybe we could go exploring," said Summer. "There's an old fort across the bridge, and it might be fun to check it out."

"That sounds interesting! But you shouldn't swim for an hour after eating. Maybe you should go exploring first," Mama said. She turned to Zinger. "And what are you and Wolf going to do?"

"Wolfie said we can play in his treehouse this afternoon. You should see it, Mama. It's really high up in the tree and there's a ladder for climbing up to it."

"Well, just be careful climbing," Mama told him. "We don't want any broken bones, do we?"

"Why do we have to wait an hour to go swimming?" Penny asked.

"Because you could get a cramp in the water. That's what my mama told me and her mama told her. So it must be true."

"What are you going to do this afternoon, Mama?" Penny asked. "Are you going to be alone?"

"No. Papa and I are going to walk through the woods, then up to the falls, and back through the village. So go and have some fun. Come back and tell us all about it."

Blackie swooped down from his favourite tree and landed on Penny's shoulder to let her know she wasn't going to get away without him.

"You're having fun, aren't you, Blackie?" Penny smiled as she stroked her feathered friend.

"Having fun! Having fun!" Blackie squawked.

The girls decided to play beach ball for a while as the net was still up, and then they would have their swim.

Penny chased Zinger down and asked him quietly, "Why didn't you tell Mama that you almost drowned?"

"Because then I would have had to tell her about Dinty and Wolfie saving me, and I didn't want to be grounded for the rest of the day. I'll tell Mama and Papa

tonight when we're around the campfire. You won't tell, will you, Penny?"

"I guess not, as long as you tell them tonight. But remember what Dinty told you and stay away from the water."

"I promise. Maybe we'll see him again before we go home. He only made himself invisible because you and the girls were coming. You should see him, Penny. He's only half as big as Wolfie and me, but he's very strong." Zinger had taken to calling his friend Wolfie.

"Well, it looks like he's keeping an eye on you, so I won't worry about you."

"So you do believe he saved me!"

"Well, somebody did, and Wolf isn't strong enough to pull you out of deep water by himself, so I guess I do believe in him. There wasn't anybody else here, was there? I believe there's magic in these woods, and magical things happen if you believe in magic."

Zinger thought his big sister was very smart. Most big people didn't believe in magic, but Penny and Summer did.

He realized what a lucky boy he was as he and Wolf ran off towards the village.

When they passed Dinty's treehouse, he slowed down and shouted as loud as he could. "Thank you, Mr. Dinty! I hope I see you again!" Then they ran like the wind along the path to the village for an afternoon of fun in Wolfie's treehouse.

The four girls played beach ball, and as usual, Blackie joined in. They took turns changing sides and partners, and nobody won because of Blackie's antics, but they had lots of fun anyway.

UNDER ATTACK

After a refreshing swim and some fun with the beach ball in the water, twisting and turning and trying to keep Blackie from zooming in on the ball, the girls got dressed and headed off in the direction of the village. They also checked out Dinty's tree as they passed, half-expecting to see the little elf. No such luck. Not even the rustle of a leaf revealed his presence.

They didn't go inside, but each gave a respectful wave, just in case Dinty or his family were watching them, invisible or not. A crowd of children followed them through the village, returning to their homes once they reached the last cabin at the edge of the village.

Summer skipped along the well-worn path and the girls trusted her to know where they were headed. But when they saw the old suspension bridge Summer expected them to cross, they felt the first trace of fear. Summer

ran lightly across and was almost to the other side when she realized that the others weren't following her.

"Come on!" she challenged them. "The bridge is safe. We use it all the time."

"Are you sure?" Penny asked. "It doesn't look very safe!"

"Dada checks it out every now and then. He checked it just last week and he said it was okay. So come on! Just stay in the middle and you'll be fine."

Penny started out first. When she told the others it seemed okay, they followed her, but their hearts were thumping in their chests until they reached the other side.

"Oh, that was scary," Penny exclaimed, and the other two girls agreed with her.

"I'm still shaking," Jillybean whispered as she offered the other girls some jellybeans.

"Me too," her sister also whispered, and she was shaking with fright. "And we have to go back over it again." The thought was almost too much for her.

"Now you are experts," Summer told them. "You won't be so scared when we go back."

"That's easy for you to say," Penny said. "You're used to it. Let's follow Summer or we'll never get there. I don't want to think about the trip back."

"Okay. It's not very far," Summer assured them. "Stay close to me, one behind the other. The path is very narrow and there are nettles and poison ivy. Just don't touch the leaves as you pass and you won't get stung."

"I don't think we should have come," Mandy whimpered.

"Oh, don't be such a baby," Penny teased her. "How can you have an adventure if you don't even try? I think this is fun. How often do we get the chance to go on a hike?"

"I suppose you're right!" Jillybean agreed. "I feel like I'm on a safari in Africa."

"Hope there aren't any lions!" Mandy murmured.

"No lions," Summer said. "But sometimes there are bears or cougars!" When she heard the yells of fright behind her, she tried to calm them down. "There haven't been any sightings for a long time. The bears and big cats like to live high in the mountains, and there has been plenty of food for them this year. They only come down near the village when they're hungry."

"That doesn't really make us feel any better," Penny said. "But let's hope there is plenty of food in the mountains like you said, or Dinty will be one busy leprechaun."

Summer didn't tell them that it was usually just the little kids that Dinty watched over. Since she didn't consider herself a little kid at eight and a half years old, she was pretty sure they were on their own. Jillybean tried not to show fear, but Mandy seemed to frighten easily, so Summer kept this information to herself.

Summer's parents didn't worry about her because they had trained her well in how to take care of herself in the woods. Even Wolfie had survival training and could fend for himself if he happened to get stranded. They knew which roots were safe to eat, how to set up a lean-to for shelter, and how to make a bed up high in the trees.

"We're almost there," she told them. "Just around the next bend, you'll be able to see the fort. Nobody has lived in it in over a hundred years, and sometimes Wolfie and I come up here with some of our friends to play Cowboys and Indians. The only difference is," she added with a giggle, "the Indians always win!"

"That's funny!" Penny laughed.

"Do you know what the fort is called?" Jillybean asked.

"Fort Danby," Summer told her. "There it is!"

The walls of the fort, though still standing, were eroded and crumbling. They could go right in without having

to climb the walls, because they had fallen down. Some of the buildings were like lean-to shanties, and their roofs had caved in. The girls were awestruck by what remained.

They were standing beside the stables when Summer suddenly became aware that they were not alone. She signalled to the girls to be quiet by putting her fingers to her lips, and then she pulled them out of sight.

They ducked behind some barrels as a man with a red bandana appeared at one of the open doors of one of the buildings. He was dirty and wore ragged clothes. The girls were ready to run when the man was joined by another man just as dirty, ragged, and untidy as the first but much fatter. Penny thought they looked familiar, but she couldn't remember where she might have noticed them before.

So far, the girls had not been seen.

"Everybody, keep quiet," Summer whispered. "I've never seen them before. Whatever you do, don't move. They must have come through the woods and sneaked around the outside of the village so nobody could see them. But why are they here?"

The girls listened quietly.

"We'll go down after dark," the first man said. "Then we'll sneak up on the campers' tent and grab the nugget. It's a good thing we were on the other side of the river when he found it. Those rushes hid us real good."

"Yea! The way they were yelling, you'd have thought they'd found the gold mine instead of just a nugget."

"It seemed to be a real big one from what I could see. It shouldn't be too hard to find. He's pretty trusting."

"We'll wait 'til everybody's asleep, then you can bonk him and his missus on the head and I'll look for the gold."

"Why don't you bonk him and the missus on the head and I'll look for the gold," the other one argued.

The girls listened to this plan in horror. "I've seen them before hanging around Papa's shop," Penny said, finally remembering. "We've got to go and warn Mama and Papa. We can't let the bandits attack them and steal their gold."

"Yes!" Summer agreed. "But we'll have to wait until they go back into the building, or they'll catch us.

Mandy choked and sobbed. "Oh, I wish I'd stayed home."

"Be quiet," Jillybean told her, "or you'll give us away." Sometimes Jillybean wondered how her twin could be so afraid of her shadow all the time.

Mandy leaned her head against the barrel, sobbing quietly to herself. Suddenly, her weight flipped the barrel forward.

The two men's heads snapped around in Mandy's direction. She was in plain sight now. Her mouth was wide open in a silent scream, and she was clearly in shock.

"Well, what have we got here?" one of the men asked. "It looks like a pretty little gal!"

Summer put her fingers to her lips. "Keep quiet," she whispered to Penny. "I'm going for help. You'd better stay with Jillybean and Mandy or they'll be scared to death. I'll be back as quickly as possible."

"Yes, go!" whispered Penny. She shielded Summer with her body as she crawled silently away on her stomach toward the back of the stable.

"Well, will you lookee here!" the man with the red bandana around his head said. He kicked the barrels aside and found not one, but three girls.

"What are you gals doin' here?" the fat man asked.

"We came to explore the fort," Penny answered.

The men hadn't noticed Summer crawling around the stable and Penny prayed that she got away. She forced herself not to look in the direction Summer had taken, hoping Mandy and Jillybean wouldn't mention that there had been another girl.

"Bring them over to the building," the man with the red bandana said. "We'd better find out how much they heard."

The men herded the girls over to the same building Penny had seen them exit. She shook her head at the girls when she noticed they were looking at her. Mandy was in tears and Jillybean was holding her sister's hand, telling her to be quiet. She hoped they understood that she didn't want them to say anything about Summer. She would do the talking.

"Put them in here!" Mr. Red Bandana said. "At least 'til I figure out what we're going to do with them."

"We just got here," Penny said, trying to be brave. "Please let us go! We don't even live here. We're out for a hike to do some exploring. We didn't know you were living here. We promise we won't tell anyone."

Her bluff didn't seem to work.

"Be quiet unless I ask a question," one man said. "Then you can talk, but not before." He motioned the other man to follow him and they both went outside.

"Don't say anything about Summer," Penny whispered to the girls. "She's gone for help. If they knew she was here, they'd go after her and we'd never get away." The girls nodded. "And stop crying, Mandy. You'll only make them mad."

Mandy sniffed twice and then stopped crying immediately.

The room was very, very dirty and there weren't any chairs to sit on, so the girls just stood and waited.

"I hope Summer got away," Penny whispered. "If she did, she should be almost home by now. She's a fast runner! And maybe Dinty will help."

Penny hoped so. Would he help kids their age? They weren't really big kids, and the longer they waited, the more scared they became.

The men returned and began to question them again.

"Why were you hiding behind the barrels?" the fat man yelled.

Penny shuffled her feet and Jillybean and Mandy stared at the ground.

"We were at the stables when we saw you," Penny said. "We're not allowed to talk to strangers. We didn't know you lived here, honest!"

"What did you hear?" Mr. Bandana shouted. "Tell me!"

"How could we hear anything from way over there?" Penny said. She had her fingers crossed behind her back.

"Don't smart-mouth me!" Mr. Bandana raised his hand to slap her, but suddenly his arm froze. "What the…?"

Penny cringed in fear, but the slap didn't land.

"Well, you're not leaving here until I know what you heard," he yelled as he tried desperately to pull his arm down with his other hand.

The girls would have laughed if they hadn't been so frightened. He suddenly stomped out of the room. His arm was still raised in the air, and he shouted frantically at the fat man. "Hey, Gus! Guard them! Don't let them out of the building!"

"Wow! What was that with the arm?" said Penny, looking bewildered. "Don't worry, girls. Summer will be home by now. Oh, that noise! What was that?"

"Just old Dinty to the rescue, Penny lass," a lilting Irish voice said.

And there he was, sitting cross-legged on the window sill, cool as a cucumber.

"Hope I didn't frighten you," Dinty said. "I came to teach these big guys a lesson. Blackie warned me you were in trouble."

"Dinty!" Penny exclaimed. "You did come! I knew you would. The bandit's arm? Was that you?"

Dinty nodded and grinned.

"But don't you only help little kids?" Penny asked.

"Sure do! You're not too big yet. Besides, you said you believed in magic, so here I am. By the way, if I suddenly vanish, it won't mean I've left you. I'll still be here."

"But how did you get here so quickly? Summer said you can't fly."

"No, but I can make myself very small, like a little field mouse, and Blackie was my chariot. I rode on his back like a gladiator to the rescue."

The girls' faces beamed. Dinty would save them!

"Summer's on her way," he said. "Now I'm going to teach these big bully boys not to pick on lovely wee colleens. So if you hear some funny stuff, it'll just be me! He-he-he...!" He chuckled merrily to himself.

Dinty disappeared, but they could still hear him chuckling. Suddenly, they heard a crash followed by a howl of pain.

"What's goin' on here?" It was Mr. Bandana's voice.

"Beats me! It felt like a mule kicked me in the face," Gus answered.

The girls grinned at each other as they heard another crash, and a scream of protest.

"Hey? Stop that! You're gonna be sorry!"

Whack! Slam!

"I didn't do it!" Gus yelped. "There's something funny going on here. Ow! Ow!" He flew past the doorway.

"Yeah! You're the one who's funny!" Mr. Bandana yelled. "I didn't know you were an acrobat. Yow! Hey! Cut that out, Gus!"

"I told you, I didn't lay a finger on you! But something is doin' a lot of damage. Ow! Ow! Something's attacking me!"

The crashing and howling went on for some time. The bandits took an awful beating, and unfortunately for them, they couldn't see their attacker.

"It's magic! That's what it is! Ow!" Mr. Bandana fell to the ground, holding his shins. "I can't take much more. I'm getting' out of here!"

"Me too!"

They both tried to run, but their legs froze.

Suddenly, Summer arrived. "There they are!" she shouted, pointing at the two bandits. "They kidnapped my friends!"

Blackie swooped in, squawking and scolding the two men. "Kidnapped! Kidnapped!" he screeched accusingly.

Dinty came back into the room with the girls. "Your daddies are here, my fine wee colleens. You have been rescued! I'm going to say goodbye now. Anytime you need me, Penny, just send Blackie for me. I've had a talk with him in bird language and he understands. I'm able to talk to all the animals. Just tell him to go find Dinty, and he'll come. Blackie and old Dinty are your protectors now because you believe in magic."

"Thanks, Dinty! You saved our lives!"

"Summer and Blackie saved you. I only gave the bandits a touch of their own medicine. I enjoyed every minute of it—and I think they'll be glad to leave. Goodbye for now, my wee friends. I'll be seeing you!"

He waved and then disappeared.

"Penny! Mandy! Jillybean!" Summer appeared at the door. "You can come out now. The bandits have been captured. Our dadas have the ropes on them and they'll be locked up for the night and taken to the sheriff in the morning."

Blackie zoomed in on the bandits and landed on Mr. Bandana's head. The bird was screeching and furiously flapping his wings. Then he zoomed onto the fat man's head and gave him the same treatment.

Penny called Blackie to come to her, and he glided over and perched gently and proudly on her shoulder. It was clear that Blackie was her protector.

The bandits babbled and blubbered in terror while Papa and Stormy questioned the girls to find out what had happened—and why the two men were so afraid of the children.

"These fellows have been beaten up pretty bad," said Papa. "Now, we know you girls couldn't have done it. So who else was here?"

"You're right, Papa!" Penny answered. "We weren't alone. Dinty Finnigan was here and he took care of us. He fought the bandits, but they couldn't see him because he was invisible, and they blamed each other, 'til they realized something else was beating them up. It was so funny, Papa! I wish you could have seen it!"

"I wish I had seen that!" said Papa. "I'll have to have a talk with Mr. Finnigan and thank him for protecting my daughter and her friends."

"Oh, he knows, Papa! He knows!" Penny said. "He's here right now. He's doing his vanishing thing, because you're not a little kid."

"Oh, I see. Well, thank you, Mr. Finnigan, wherever you are!" Papa saluted and the girls giggled.

Blackie swooped with excitement now that Penny was safe, and then he perched on her shoulder once more. Penny stroked his feathers and gave him a peck on the beak to thank him for helping save her and the girls.

"Penny loves Blackie," she said.

Blackie soared happily back into the air, chattering as he flew. "Penny loves Blackie, Penny loves Blackie."

He kept squawking like this for the whole trip back, keeping the girls in fits of giggles.

•

That night, around the campfire, was the best time of all. They were happy, but also a bit sad, because the Henrys

86

and Jillybean and Mandy would be leaving in the morning. Zinger told his parents about Dinty and Wolfie saving his life, and Penny told them about her scary adventure.

"Dinty said that if I ever need him, all I have to do is send Blackie and he will come immediately. Dinty and Blackie make a great team. Don't you think so, Mama?"

"I certainly do!" Mama agreed.

"Blackie flew home with me," Summer told them. "He didn't make a sound until we got away from the fort, and then he never stopped screeching. It's no wonder Dinty heard him before we arrived at the village."

Penny was going to miss Summer, but Papa promised they would be back again in a couple of weeks. And Summer promised that next time her dada went to Green Oaks for supplies, she and Wolfie would go with him.

NEXT IN THE *PENELOPE HENRY* SERIES:

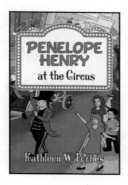

At the Circus

Penelope's world turns upside-down with the arrival of the circus in her normally quiet village of Green Oaks. Just in case that's not exciting enough, it's also her ninth birthday!

When a monkey escapes from the circus and gets into a tangle with one of Penelope's friends, the circus owner invites them all to see the show—for free. All of Penelope's dreams come true when she is chosen to participate in one of the circus's most exciting acts.

But trouble strikes when the lions get out of their enclosure and the elephant trainer mysteriously goes missing, threatening the entire circus. Will the show be able to go on? With the help of Dinty the leprechaun, Penelope and her new friends are sure to have their hands full.

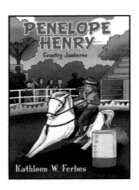

Country Jamboree

Country Jamboree will take you on a weekend of fun for the whole family. Join Penelope and her family and friends down on the farm for a rodeo with their country cousins where they'll watch the horse racing, the chuck wagons, and trick riding! Encounter mystery and discovery with surprises around every corner. Although facing danger and uncertainty, Penelope and friends are protected by Dinty Finnigan, the Irish leprechaun who protects small children and brings fun and magic everywhere he goes. Penelope and her friends will guide you on adventures great and small as they explore the farm and all the fun to be had!

ALSO AVAILABLE BY KATHLEEN FORBES:

All Roads Lead to Home
978-1-4866-0789-1

Kathleen has discovered something magical in every province of this grand country, Canada. She sees the beauty in God's gifts to us: the mountains, the valleys, the trees, and the rivers and lakes, which have all inspired her poetry. Most poems are spiritual, some are for children, and some are just plain silly. Come and journey through the hills of Ireland, the cities of Ontario, and the majestic mountains of British Columbia with Kathleen's poetry. She hopes you find something to warm your heart.

The Holly Brannigan Mystery Series:

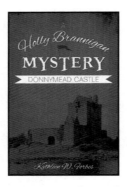

Donnymead Castle
978-1-4866-0801-0

Follow the exciting adventures of teen amateur sleuth Holly Brannigan, the daughter of Detective David Brannigan.

When Holly and her family visit Holly's grandmother in her cottage on the grounds of Donnymead Castle, Holly is fascinated with the castle and manages to talk the caretaker into giving her a tour. But mysterious activity has been taking place on the castle grounds and Holly will have to put her sleuthing skills to the test.

Join Holly and her friend Tim on their explorations of the ancient village. Trace the threads of history from the past into the future and follow Holly and Tim as they discover that things aren't always as they appear. As the mystery deepens, Holly and Tim become lost in history, but can they discover who is behind the criminal activity in Donnymead?

Scuba Hijinks
978-1-4866-0805-8

Scuba Hijinks is the second book in the *Holly Brannigan Mystery* series. Set on the West Coast of Canada in the Lions Bay and Porteau Bay area, the story follows the adventures of teen sleuth Holly Brannigan and her friends, Bonnie, Paul, and Ted as they team up with Holly's father, Detective David Brannigan, to catch a gang of rogue scuba divers. Holly and her friends learn to scuba dive in order to pursue the criminals, and they bravely face challenges and dangers throughout the case. Thrust into a world of kidnapping and vandalism, the amateur detectives use their new skills and unlimited trust in each other to bring the gang to justice.

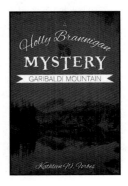

Garibaldi Mountain
978-1-4866-1124-9

Holly Brannigan and her three teenage friends–Paul Castles, Ted Lumley, and her best friend, Bonnie Tilson–have helped attorney David Brannigan, Holly's father, on cases in the past, but this is the most dangerous mystery yet. A family with three children has disappeared, along with a close friend of the family, while camping in Garibaldi Provincial Park. When Holly and her friends hear of the disaster, they join a Mountain Search and Rescue team of volunteers to help the search. In very short order, Holly's team find clues that make them suspicious of foul play.

Follow Holly and her team as they search through torrential rain and fog, confront a dangerous wolf and its pack, and dodge men with bows and arrows who are terrorizing them as they race the clock to find the missing family. There are new threats and dangers at every turn!

A Holly Brannigan Mystery: Garibaldi Mountain is the third in the series.